Pebble®
Bilingüe/
Bilingual Plus

Comida sana con MiPirámide /Healthy Eating with MyPyramid
El grupo de las frutas/The Fruit Group

por/by Mari C. Schuh

Traducción/Translation: Dr. Martín Luis Guzmán Ferrer
Editor Consultor/Consulting Editor: Dra. Gail Saunders-Smith

Consultor/Consultant: Barbara J. Rolls, PhD
Guthrie Chair in Nutrition
The Pennsylvania State University
University Park, Pennsylvania

Capstone
press®

Mankato, Minnesota

Pebble Plus is published by Capstone Press,
151 Good Counsel Drive, P.O. Box 669, Mankato, Minnesota 56002.
www.capstonepress.com

1 2 3 4 5 6 11 10 09 08 07 06

Library of Congress Cataloging-in-Publication Data
Schuh, Mari C., 1975–
   [Fruit group. English & Spanish]
   El grupo de las frutas = The fruit group/de/by Mari C. Schuh.
   p. cm.—(Comida sana con MiPirámide = Healthy eating with MyPyramid)
   Includes index.
   Parallel text in English and Spanish.
   ISBN-13: 978-0-7368-6666-8 (hardcover)
   ISBN-10: 0-7368-6666-3 (hardcover)
   1. Fruit—Juvenile literature. 2. Nutrition—Juvenile literature. I. Title.
TX558.F7S3818 2007
641.3'4—dc22   2005037165

Summary: Simple text and photographs present the fruit group, the foods in this group, and examples of
       healthy eating choices—in both English and Spanish.

Credits
Katy Kudela, bilingual editor; Eida del Risco, Spanish copy editor; Jennifer Bergstrom, designer;
       Kelly Garvin, photo researcher; Stacy Foster and Michelle Biedscheid, photo shoot coordinators

Photo Credits
Capstone Press/Karon Dubke, cover, 1, 5, 9, 11, 13, 15, 16–17, 19, 21, 22 (all)
Corbis/Claude Woodruff, 6–7; Michael Prince, 5 (background)
U.S. Department of Agriculture, 8, 9 (inset)

**Information in this book supports the U.S. Department of Agriculture's MyPyramid for Kids
food guidance system found at http://www.MyPyramid.gov/kids. Food amounts listed in this
book are based on an 1,800-calorie food plan.**

**The U.S. Department of Agriculture (USDA) does not endorse any products, services,
or organizations.**

Note to Parents and Teachers

The Comida sana con MiPirámide/Healthy Eating with MyPyramid set supports national
science standards related to nutrition and physical health. This book describes the fruit
group in both English and Spanish. The images support early readers in understanding the
text. The repetition of words and phrases helps early readers learn new words. This book
also introduces early readers to subject-specific vocabulary words, which are defined in
the Glossary section. Early readers may need assistance to read some words and to use the
Table of Contents, Glossary, Internet Sites, and Index sections of the book.

Table of Contents

Tabla de contenidos

Fruit

Fruit helps keep you
healthy and strong.
What fruit have
you eaten today?

Las frutas

Las frutas te ayudan
a estar sano y fuerte.
¿Qué fruta has comido hoy?

Do you ever wonder
where fruit comes from?
Fruit grows on trees,
bushes, and vines.

¿Alguna vez te has preguntado
de dónde vienen las frutas?
Las frutas crecen en los árboles,
arbustos y enredaderas.

MyPyramid for Kids

MyPyramid teaches you how much to eat from each food group. Fruit is a food group in MyPyramid.

MiPirámide para niños

MiPirámide te enseña cuánto debes comer de cada uno de los grupos de alimentos. El grupo de las frutas es parte de MiPirámide.

MyPyramid For Kids
Eat Right. Exercise. Have Fun.

To learn more about healthy eating, go to this web site: www.MyPyramid.gov/kids Ask an adult for help.

Para saber más sobre comida sana, ve a este sitio de Internet: www.MyPyramid.gov/kids Pídele a un adulto que te ayude.

Kids should eat
about 1½ cups of fruit
every day.

Los chicos deben comer
como 1½ tazas de
fruta todos los días.

Enjoying Fruit

Yellow, orange, red.

How many colors can you eat?

Enjoy bananas, oranges,

and apples.

Cómo disfrutar de las frutas

Amarillo, anaranjado, rojo.

¿Cuántos colores puedes comerte?

Disfruta los plátanos, las naranjas

y las manzanas.

Pears, melons, grapefruit.
Fruit comes in
many shapes and sizes.
Try a fruit you've never
eaten before.

Peras, melones y toronjas.
Las frutas son de muchas
formas y tamaños. Prueba una
fruta que nunca hayas comido.

Strawberries make
a good snack
to share with a friend.

Las fresas son una buena
merienda para compartir
con una amiga.

Sip, slurp, gulp.
Enjoy a cold fruit smoothie.
Smoothies have lots of fruit
in them.

Da unos sorbitos.
Disfruta un licuado
de fruta frío. Los licuados
contienen mucha fruta.

Fruit makes a sweet part
of a healthy lunch.
What are your favorite fruits?

La fruta puede ser el postre
después un almuerzo sano.
¿Cuáles son tus frutas preferidas?

How Much to Eat/Cuánto hay que comer

Kids need to eat about 1½ cups of fruit every day. To get 1½ cups, pick three of your favorite fruits below.

Los niños necesitan 1½ tazas de fruta todos los días. Para completar 1½ tazas, escoge tres de tus frutas preferidas.

Pick three of your favorite fruits to enjoy today!

¡Escoge tres de tus frutas preferidas para disfrutarlas hoy!

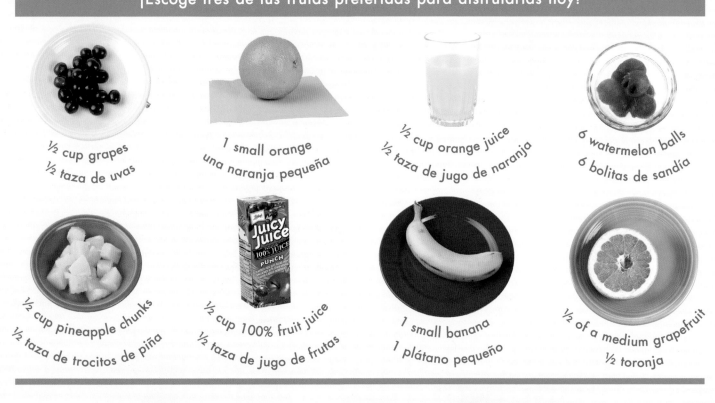

½ cup grapes
½ taza de uvas

1 small orange
una naranja pequeña

½ cup orange juice
½ taza de jugo de naranja

6 watermelon balls
6 bolitas de sandía

½ cup pineapple chunks
½ taza de trocitos de piña

½ cup 100% fruit juice
½ taza de jugo de frutas

1 small banana
1 plátano pequeño

½ of a medium grapefruit
½ toronja

½ cup/taza   +   ½ cup/taza   +   ½ cup/taza   =   1½ cups/tazas

Glossary

fruit—the fleshy, juicy part of a plant; fruit has seeds.

MyPyramid—a food plan that helps kids make healthy food choices and reminds kids to be active; MyPyramid was created by the U.S. Department of Agriculture.

smoothie—a thick, smooth drink made by mixing milk, low-fat yogurt, and fruit in a blender

Glosario

la fruta—parte carnosa y jugosa de una planta; la fruta tiene semillas.

el licuado—bebida espesa y suave hecha en licuadora mezclando leche, yogurt bajo en grasas y frutas

MiPirámide—plan de alimentos que ayuda a los chicos a escoger comidas saludables y a mantenerse activos; MiPirámide fue creada por el Departamento de Agricultura de los Estados Unidos.

Index

Internet Sites

FactHound offers a safe, fun way to find Internet sites related to this book. All of the sites on FactHound have been researched by our staff.

Here's how:

1. Visit *www.facthound.com*

2. Choose your grade level.

3. Type in this book ID **0736866663** for age-appropriate sites. You may also browse subjects by clicking on letters, or by clicking on pictures and words.

4. Click on the **Fetch It** button.

FactHound will fetch the best sites for you!

Índice

Sitios de Internet

FactHound proporciona una manera divertida y segura de encontrar sitios de Internet relacionados con este libro. Nuestro personal ha investigado todos los sitios de FactHound. Es posible que los sitios no estén en español.

Se hace así:

1. Visita *www.facthound.com*

2. Elige tu grado escolar.

3. Introduce este código especial **0736866663** para ver sitios apropiados según tu edad, o usa una palabra relacionada con este libro para hacer una búsqueda general.

4. Haz clic en el botón **Fetch It**.

¡FactHound buscará los mejores sitios para ti!